Contents

Chapter One   7

Chapter Two   15

Chapter Three   23

Chapter Four   29

Chapter Five   37

Chapter Six   49

Chapter Seven   59

Chapter Eight   67

Chapter Nine   83

PART ONE
SAINT-DOMINGUE

Chapter One

October 1775, Jeremie

"Benedict has always been free!" I glared at the new boy, Pierre. I did not shout. I tried to make my voice sound like his foul words didn't matter.

My friends on the beach had skin of all colours, some lighter, some darker than mine. We all came here most days when the sun was cooler, to ride our horses on the sand. There were Dan and Henri, who were fishermen's sons. And Georges and Jean, whose fathers, like mine, ran coffee farms. Benedict, who was darkest of all, had a mother who ran a bar on the main street; he had better clothes than any of us, but never made any fuss about it.

"Well, you are all no *better* than slaves." Pierre sat tall in his saddle and looked round at the group. "In France, we call you scum."

"Shut up, Pierre!" Benedict kicked his horse into a trot and rode away down the beach. Pierre Despard, his face ham-pink from the sun, started laughing.

I pulled my horse, Merle, round to face him. "You think you are better than us?"

"Naturally. My father owns people like you. This horse cost more than any of you would fetch at market. I expect even my boots—"

"You know what?" I said. I was fed up with this boy. "I will make a bet with you. I bet my horse can beat yours to the rocks and back."

He sneered.

Merle began to dance around. She could tell I was upset and snorted at me to calm down. I took a deep breath, settled myself. Pierre's horse looked expensive, it was the colour of the finest pastry and its mane and tail were white as sea foam. But I knew my Merle was faster. My father had given me Merle when I was seven, taught me how to train her, how to ride. I was nearly fourteen now. Merle and I had grown together, learned to work together as smoothly as if we shared the same breath. I knew she could beat him. She might not look as smart, but she would do anything for me.

Pierre said nothing for a long minute.

"Are you chicken?" Jean and Georges made clucking noises.

"Of course not!" Pierre turned his horse around. "I cannot lose!"

The wind whipped in from the sea and blew up some sand. It stung my eyes a little and it must have stung Pierre's horse too because she suddenly reared up on her hind legs. For a moment I thought he might fall – in fact it was hard not to enjoy the fear that flickered across his face. Some of the others laughed and we could all see just how angry that made him.

"You cannot best me!" Pierre spat, and kicked his horse on into a gallop.

He was at least four strides ahead of me, but I knew Merle could catch them.

"*Allez!*" I called, and Merle's ears pricked forward and she almost flew.

The sound of her hooves matched the sound of my heart. The sand flicked up with every step and the sea glittered silver. To my left, the hills of the island were the brightest green, and above, the blue of the sky was so bright you could not look at it for long. Merle stretched out even faster and I flattened myself against her back.

We overtook easily. I heard Pierre swear all the worst words I'd ever heard.

Up ahead a log lay directly in our path, half in and half out of the water. I gave Merle a tiny squeeze and she took off, leaping up into the air and across the log. I would tell Papa about this when I got home, I thought; how high Merle had jumped, how fast she had run.

We'd almost reached the rocks when I heard a shout. I didn't look round at first, Pierre was full of tricks and I would not put it past him to cheat. To make it seem he was the winner whatever happened. But when I did look, it was as if the log had come to life. His horse reared again, swung round and screamed. If you have ever heard a horse screaming you will know it is a terrible sound.

I could see now that it was not a log. It was a caiman, longer than a man, snapping its huge jaws and thrashing its massive tail. Its teeth, I swear, were white and shining, and each one was as big as my forearm.

"Pierre!" I yelled. I hated the boy, but no one deserved to be eaten alive.

The other boys were all far away down the other end of the beach. I cupped my hands and yelled. "Serpentine!" I waved my hands like a snake. Pierre did not see. He did not even look at me. He and the horse were frozen with fear as the caiman's jaws snapped closer and closer.

If I did nothing there would be no horse and no Pierre.

I leaned forward and whispered into Merle's ears. "Come on." I felt her hesitate; she was afraid. I could feel her heart, fluttery under her ribs, beating ten to the dozen. But I squeezed her on, and we rode straight towards the boy and the horse and the snapping monster.

Without breaking stride, I leaned across as I got close and took his horse's bridle in my hand, pulling the terrified animal away from the caiman and leading it in a zigzag motion over the sand. The caiman tried to follow. Travelling in a straight line, those things can propel themselves up and down the beach faster than lightning, but side to side they are lumbering and slow.

Pierre was still praying when we reached the others and had almost stopped shaking. His perfect horse was rolling its eyes, its flanks heaving as it gulped down air. It would not stay still, and pranced and danced around. I thanked Merle with a pat and jumped down from the saddle to hold Pierre's horse. I sang soothing words in its ears, the words Papa had taught me from when he was a cavalry officer in the French army.

The horse calmed, tossing its head and nuzzling me. I smiled, I may not have a friend in Pierre but at least his mount appreciated me.

Suddenly all I heard was laughter. Pierre was laughing at me.

"Jungle boy!" he said, and at first I thought I hadn't heard him properly. "Are you speaking to my horse? Is it only animals that understand you?"

Henri was angry on my behalf. "Hey! Thomas beat you! He beat you and then he saved your life!"

Pierre scoffed. "He did it on purpose. He led me to that creature. I would have caught him if he hadn't. It was his fault. He could have killed me!"

I would have hit him then, but Henri held me back. "It's not worth it," he said quietly. I shook him off.

"You may look like a gentleman," I said, "but you are nothing."

Pierre looked down at me from the saddle.

"You are Antoine Delisle's son?" He said it as if I were a piece of rotting filth and not a boy. And he was sneering too. "Soon you will have nothing and you will be nobody." He took the reins and trotted away.

I was seething. I shouted after him, "You know nothing about me! About my family!"

"He's all mouth, that one," Henri said. But he did not look at me when he said it and I could not help feeling a shiver of worry. Papa had been too busy to be himself these past weeks. The last harvest had been poor. We all needed new shoes. And Papa had stopped teaching the little ones the Greek and Latin he taught me. He said they wouldn't need it – that no one needed any learning out here.

I shook those bad thoughts away. I told myself I would stop off at Maman's grave on the way home and tell her my worries. Then they would float away up into the blue sky and be forgotten.

Chapter Two

Maman's grave was at the side of the churchyard on the hill outside town, a mile and a half from our farm. I tied Merle up outside the church and hopped over the low wall, then spent a good fifteen minutes clearing the plants from the grave.

"Papa will buy you a stone soon, Maman," I told her. "I made him promise."

I moved the creeper from where I had carved her name: Marie Cessette Dumas Delisle.

The sound of the tree frogs and the hum of the insects filled the air.

It was two years now. I wondered if the little ones could even remember her. I ought to tell them the story of how she had chased Papa's old dog when it stole his tartine. And how she had made the best cornmeal, and had known where the best custard apples grew.

I decided that if Papa was in a good mood when I was home, I'd fetch some of the brandy he liked from the bottle hidden in the outside kitchen at the back of our yard, and I would remind him about the gravestone.

When I did get home, the sun was dipping down over the coconut palms and the light was fading. The long branches of the palms made dark ribbons of moving blue shadow all across our front yard. Up on the veranda, Papa was talking to the coffee factor, the man with a squashed three-cornered hat who bought our beans and roasted them. But the harvest was over, and I thought it odd that he was here now. I went to ask my littlest brother Charles what was happening, but he was busy in the dirt making a pile of stones into a little farm, with pebbles for horses and melon seeds for goats.

"What's happening, Charlot?" I asked.

"Papa says we are going away," he said, and made one of his pebble horses jump high in the air. "Where are we going, Thomas?"

I was suddenly worried again, but I kept my voice steady. "No one is going anywhere."

I went to put Merle in her stable. The saddle was flecked with saltwater where we'd galloped through the waves. I ought to take it in and clean it.

I was walking back to the house when I saw the coffee factor lead Charles and my sister Berthe and my other brother, Petit Antoine, away. Berthe had to pull Charles away from his toy farm, and he grizzled as they climbed up into the cart. But they waved at me, smiling, as the cart pulled out on to the track that led back into town. So I waved back. Berthe and Antoine sometimes went to help with fruit picking, but I wondered what good Charles would do, surely he would only cry and get in the way.

In the house, Papa was cleaning his best boots on the veranda. His ancient travelling trunk had been pulled out by the steps. It was older than me and had come, along with Papa, from France, when he had first been posted here with the army.

I put the saddle down close by and started washing off the saltwater and sweat. Papa nodded hello but he didn't turn his attention away from his careful, methodical work for more than a moment. I looked at him sideways. Sometimes talking to Papa was like approaching a skittish horse – you had to do it in a roundabout way.

He was old, my father, nearer the age of most boys' grandfathers, but he was still strong, his white skin tanned and freckled from the sun and almost as creased and leathery as those boots. He had sharp grey eyes, like the stones at the bottom of a river, shiny and hard, but when he smiled, when I showed him how well I'd come on with my Latin, or how straight

I could shoot a pistol, or how I took care of Merle, kindness would flood his face.

So, after a while, I set aside the saddle and fetched the brandy; then I would bring up the gravestone, I thought. That was always best with Papa. He was a bit like a caiman; he could be snappy.

"Should I fetch them tomorrow?" I asked as I poured him a measure. "The little ones?"

Papa took the brandy and gulped it down, but didn't reply. I refilled his glass and set it down close by, then went back to cleaning the saddle: small circles with a soft cloth, making the leather shine like new. He drank the second measure in one go and gasped with the sting of it. Maybe the brandy would take a while to work.

Papa lifted his old cavalry sabre from the ancient trunk and took it out of the scabbard. I loved that sabre. It looked as good as new. The tassels that hung from the handle had not lost their colour; they shone scarlet as new bougainvillea flowers.

"One day, Thomas," he said, "this sabre will be yours." He smiled, but he wasn't looking at me.

I had to get his attention. "We won the race today, Merle and me..."

"Merle and I," he snapped.

"Merle and I," I corrected myself, and went back to polishing. Tonight would not be a good time to ask about Mama's stone after all, I realised. I would finish cleaning the saddle and go to bed. I sighed, but quietly.

Papa cleared his throat, poured himself more brandy. "I have been meaning to tell you, Thomas." He gave the sabre a long look, checking the blade was still true. "I have sold the estate."

I felt my insides turn over. I must have heard him wrong.

"Excuse me, Papa?" My voice was small.

"The house, the fields. Things have not been well, not since your mother..." He slid the sword back into its cover and put it away in the trunk.

"I am too old to be a coffee farmer." He waved an insect away from his face. "It is time to go home."

Papa was talking as if what he had said was the most ordinary thing in the world. But Saint-Domingue was my home; our home. The only home I could remember. Our farm, from the side of the hill to the top where the coffee berries grew, from the stream that flowed through our land on the way to the sea to the road that led into town. My mind was racing. I wanted to shout, to yell. But I kept quiet.

"There is a ship leaving Port-au-Prince at the end of the week. We will ride north, you and I, in the morning." He said it so matter of fact, as if he was telling me to look to the fence around the goat pen, or finish my Greek homework.

I felt my throat so tight I could not speak. Suddenly all I could hear was the blood rushing around my head. Not the insects or the frogs, not the night birds or the wind swishing around the leaves of the trees around the house.

Papa had got up. He'd gone inside and lit a candle, and I was alone on the veranda.

I didn't sleep at all.

Papa had told us about the winters in Normandy, the part of France where he'd grown up; about living in an old stone castle and getting so cold his skin turned blue. Would I turn blue too? Pierre had said yesterday that they didn't let free people of colour into France. I imagined me and the little ones stuck on a boat in the cold. I rolled over. There was another worry: why had Papa sent my siblings away?

I don't remember when it finally began to grow light, but the cockerel in the yard suddenly called loud and jagged. I got up to feed him for the last time.

What would happen to Maman's grave now? I hoped perhaps I would have time to make one last visit, but there was too much to do. The carrier came for Papa's trunk, and as I helped load it on to the cart, I thought that in one year, perhaps two, no one would even know the grave was there. The trees and the creepers and the yellow flowers would grow right over it.

There would never be a gravestone now, and no one would remember her.

Chapter Three

Port-au-Prince

Me and Papa left after breakfast. I had a small bag with my best clothes rolled up tight, and a pebble from the bottom of the stream, one I had found years ago when I was little and bothered with pebbles. I had the knife Papa had given me too, and I should have liked to take the head collar I'd made for Merle out of rope but Papa said we would not need it.

"When will we meet up with Charles and the others?" I asked. But Papa simply changed the subject.

"There are things you do not know about me, Thomas-Alexandre." We were on the road out of Jeremie that followed the coast to the north. He looked out at the sea as if he could see things I couldn't.

I said nothing.

"I am not Antoine Delisle. That is not my name."

"What do you mean?" I pushed Merle on and rode alongside him. "You are not my father?"

He laughed then. "No, I am your father, that is true. But what I am about to tell you is also true."

He took a deep breath. "I am a marquis, the Marquis Alexandre Antoine Davy de la Pailleterie." He sighed then. "And you, Thomas-Alexandre, you are a count."

My mouth was flapping open, I swear a fly hit the back of my throat. Merle stumbled and I was still so stunned I almost slid off.

He nodded. "You understand, my son? The boat is waiting, I must claim what is mine. And yours."

Every night when we stopped at an inn, Papa talked about France, how with his land and castle there, there would be more money than I could imagine. How the hills were a different green to our own, with different trees.

"And none of these damn insects!"

He said nothing about the little ones. It was as if they didn't exist. I told myself we'd catch up with them at the next inn, or perhaps on the boat.

On the fourth day, though, as we rode down the hill into the city of Port-au-Prince, the capital of our island, I am ashamed to say that the sight of the city almost put all thoughts of my siblings from my mind. The place was much bigger than Jeremie, which was the only town I had ever seen, but it was not as grand. We had an opera house and enough people with fine clothes and money to spend to go there – I had

24

only visited once, but it had been like magic. Here in Port-au-Prince, though, there were lines of African slaves shackled and weeping. I saw an auction too, and wondered if that was how Papa had bought Maman? I think the feeling in my bones was fear, and I was not used to it.

As we rode, Merle tossed her mane and whisked her tail. She could tell something was not right and I knew, like me, she was not happy being so far from home. I leaned forward and whispered into her ears that it would be all right. I made sure not to promise, though, in case it was another promise I could not keep.

The harbour was full of boats. So many boats! All with tall masts, like a forest of dead trees that had been struck by lightning and lost their leaves. We tied up the horses and Papa told me to make Merle tidy and presentable.

"The horses are sold already." He said it matter of fact, as if he had told me already and I had forgotten.

"Not Merle!" My voice shook. But Papa simply nodded.

I thought then that perhaps I should mount up and ride my horse back out of town and home again. I was nearly fourteen, I could ride and shoot and knew when you should pick and plant coffee.

What had I been thinking! I was sleepwalking! Of course Merle would not be coming. The boat to France took six weeks and she might hate it, might jump overboard and drown. But I had been trying my best not to think about it. I had known Merle for half my life; she was as much a part of me as my arm.

"Thomas!" Papa's voice snapped me back to attention. I sniffed. I knew my lip was trembling. Then he leaned down. He was a tall man and he put his hand on my shoulder. "I know this is hard, my boy," he said. "I know what she means to you, but it must be done. We sail tomorrow. There will be other horses in France. Finer ones." He looked at me then too, and I blinked and wiped my face. "Good lad," he said and patted my shoulder. "Be brave." He smiled.

I felt like my throat had closed up tight. I blinked again.

"Harden your heart," Papa said. "Be a man." I tried to nod. But I was thinking, if this is what it felt like being a man, I would rather be a horse.

I went to Merle, brushed her and combed out her mane one last time. She snorted and nudged me with her head. I threw my arms round her neck and hugged her tight, and she rested the weight of her head against me.

"Courage," I whispered, then I put my eye right up to hers. "Remember me, my friend." I hoped she would.

Across the street I saw a boy – smaller, skinnier and darker skinned than me – cross the road towards the docks, pushing a trolley piled high with trunks. He dodged a cart and the trunks fell. I thought to run and help him, but at once a large white man waded into the road and beat him hard with a long stick. I could hear the sound of the stick cracking against the boy's back but he did not cry out. Not once.

I thanked my stars I was born free.

Chapter Four

That night Papa stayed up late. I woke up once and realised he was not in the room we shared. I was worried then, and got out of bed, put on my good jacket and trousers and crept to the top of the stairs. In the saloon down below, all the men except the waiters were white. I heard Papa first; he was at a card table playing with a man wearing shiny buttons. I could tell Papa had drunk too much, and it did not look like the game was going his way. I watched as he stood up, angry, pushing the table over and swearing the very worst words. Papa pulled out his cavalry sword, and for a moment I thought there would be a duel.

"Papa!" I could not help shouting. He looked up and saw me, and I felt worse than ever. My papa was more than drunk. His shirt was stained and he swayed as he walked. I went over and he leaned on me.

The man with the buttons was smirking. Up close he reminded me of Pierre Despard, the boy on the beach.

"Monsieur Delisle!" he said sharply. "I trust you will find the money you owe me before your boat sails?"

Papa almost growled. "Do you doubt me?"

I led him away. I did not like to remind Papa that we had no money apart from what had come from the sale of the horses. Papa had promised we would be rich in France. But France was still six weeks away.

Before he fell into bed I asked about my brothers and sister, about Charles and Petit Antoine and Berthe. "Will they be on the boat tomorrow, Papa?" I said.

"*Non*," he said and rolled over, pulling the blanket over his head. "They have gone to the coffee factor to cover the debts."

My stomach swooped into my boots.

Debts? I'd had no idea. But before I could take it in, Papa had already begun to snore.

In the morning I was still angry. My whole family had gone. Merle and the little ones... Would they end up like that boy in the street? Beaten for nothing? Slaves forever? Berthe was too clever to get hit so hard, but Charles? How would he survive? I shut my eyes tight. I blinked again.

Papa asked for coffee and I fetched it slower than a turtle waddling up the beach. I came back up and slammed it down next to him. Papa was still suffering from the drink but I didn't care.

"You sold them!" I could not stay silent. "You sold Merle and you sold my brothers and sister!"

He was not moved by my fury. He opened the shutters and tilted his face up to catch the warm sun as if my words were nothing. "Be quiet, Thomas. I am your father," he said without looking at me. "If you want to become a count, you will do as I say."

I slammed out of the inn and into the street. Merle was already gone. If she had still been there I would have leaped on her back and ridden like the wind back to Jeremie. I did not want to be a count. I did not want to go to France.

The boat we were to sail on was called the *Glory*. She was bigger than the biggest house I had ever seen. Up high in the forest of her masts – I counted three massive ones and two smaller – I saw a boy my age, walking barefoot along the yardarm as sure-footedly as I would have walked on solid ground. The idea of asking for a place on another boat flew into my head. I was good at climbing, I could make myself useful on a ship. At that moment I thought I would not be happy unless I was as far away from Papa as possible.

My papa. He was an idiot. The biggest idiot in all the island. In all France! I kicked a stone and it flew off the quay and plopped into the sea. I was being foolish,

I knew. I would not be better off boarding some ship and sailing away to God-knows-where – either way I would be forced to leave my home behind. Maybe there would be some future for me in France after all.

At that moment Papa stood on the steps of the inn and shouted for me. For a few moments I hesitated. Where could I go? What could I do? I sighed, then made my way back through the traffic of men and horses and carts. I found Papa inside with the shiny-buttoned card player. He looked terrible. I could smell the rum in his sweat.

"Captain Langlois, this is Thomas-Alexandre," Papa said tapping me on the shoulder. I stood up straight and nodded, the way I'd been taught.

Captain Langlois looked me up and down. I felt slightly uncomfortable. He looked at me in the same way the man who'd bought Merle had looked at her.

"Fourteen? Costs a lot to feed and water no doubt." Captain Langlois didn't speak to me but to Papa, who nodded. "Tall for his age."

"I am fourteen next year, sir," I added. I was proud of being tall. That morning it was perhaps the only thing I had got from Papa I was glad to have.

Captain Langlois smiled and nodded. "One thousand livres, you say?" Papa nodded. I looked at him; he could not meet my eyes. A terrible sense of foreboding began to creep into my gut.

"Six hundred, Antoine," Captain Langlois said. "I am a businessman."

Papa passed his hand across his face. "See here, Captain. I lost the money for the passage home last night. I cannot afford to go lower than eight hundred." He pointed his finger, jabbing it at the tabletop. "I will, of course, redeem the boy once my inheritance..."

Captain Langlois waved him to stop. "I cannot wait for money that may or may not..."

Papa's voice had an edge of despair. He was sweating. "The boy is my son!"

Captain Langlois put his hand out to shake Papa's. "Eight hundred, then."

Papa hesitated. Then the men shook hands.

I stood bolt upright as Captain Langlois counted out eight hundred livres in bank notes and handed them to Papa. Now I understood. He was selling me. He had just sold me.

He had sold the coffee farm, the house with its white-painted veranda and vegetable garden. He had sold my two little brothers and my one sister. His own flesh and blood. He had sold my horse.

I was burning with anger. I looked from one man to the other. Papa took me by both shoulders, kissed me on both cheeks. "Be brave," he whispered. "I will send for you." I tried to pull away but he gripped my shoulder tight. "I *will* send for you. And I will be a marquis and you, my son, will be a count."

He wiped his eyes. Was he crying? I hoped so. I wished I could have spat in his face, but my throat was dry as sand at midday.

My eyes were dry as well. I had no tears for this man. He did not deserve them.

I walked out of that inn with Captain Langlois and did not look back.

I was no longer free.

PART TWO
FRANCE

Chapter Five

October 1777, St Germain-en-Laye,
Northern France

I stepped off the ship behind the captain. The sun was high, but it was not as hot as home; there was a sharp wind from the sea that seemed to cut through me. After nearly two months aboard ship, dry land felt strange; hard and unmoving under my feet. In my hand held tight was the tiny pebble from the river at home, the only thing left of my old life.

I had spent half a year as a slave. I knew I had been lucky in many respects. I had not worked on a sugar plantation, forced to cut cane from first light, or in the refineries that burned night and day. I never had to wear shackles or chains and I had a bed to sleep on, rather than the floor. But I knew every second, every moment of every day that I was not free. I tried looking for my family, and heard only bad news or no news. I looked for Merle, but she was long gone.

I had given up thinking my father would send for me. I had given up on everything. I learned to keep my mouth shut and my face blank.

The man at the customs office waved his quill pen towards me as he spoke to the captain. "This boy is yours?"

The captain nodded. "I am delivering him to the Marquis Alexandre Antoine Davy de la Pailleterie."

The customs officer stood up and looked at me. I was at least a head and shoulders taller than him. And I was taller than Captain Langlois. For the first time in half a year I drew myself up as tall as I could and looked a man straight in the eyes. I was more than their equal. Very soon I would be Comte Thomas-Alexandre Dumas Davy de la Pailleterie, and no one would own me ever again.

I took the coach to the address my father had given me. I remembered him telling me about his castle, his land, but instead of a sprawling estate I arrived at a tall gleaming whitewashed house in a new town west of Paris. There were four floors, with windows either side on each one. My father was waiting for me in front of the shiny black door, but at first I barely recognised him. He looked much older than I remembered, paler skinned now and dressed in such fine clothes. I kept my face, just as I had done as a slave, stony still.

"Thomas-Alexandre!" There was a kind of catch in his voice. "You cannot know how much I have missed you."

I nodded, like the footman I had been to Captain Langlois. I would not give him any credit for saving me.

"Come, come, my boy! I have so much to show you – not the castle, no." He put a finger to his lips as if he was about to tell a secret. "I have mortgaged it! I thought you and I would do better with... Come, let me show you."

He led me to the stables at the back of the house. That was what he had meant, then, I thought, when he had said there was money here in France; there had been no money, only land he had been able to sell... As we came to the stables, though, my attention was seized by the sight of a magnificent grey horse, saddled and ready. "He is yours, my boy. All yours. I do believe you have earned him. His name is Gunsmoke."

I hate to admit it, but my father close to won me over with money. It wasn't only the horse, who moved like a dream; it was the clothes, the fine jacket, the embroidered waistcoat and the black leather riding boots, so shiny I could see my face in them.

In my time as a slave, and then on the boat, I had imagined the things I would say to him. The curses I would bring down on his head. Now, seeing him so keen to please, I felt almost sorry for him. I could not help it. I threw my arms round him. He was, after all, the only family I had.

Father took me to Paris, a few hours away by coach, and showed me off. We visited the theatre, the shops. He bought me a fine sword with a silk tassel to hang from my belt. I must admit it felt good in my hand, light as driftwood and gleaming when it caught the light. I wished I could have shown it to my friends back on the beach at Jeremie. They would never have believed their eyes.

Father promised to enrol me in a military academy, where I would learn how to use it properly, and he kept his promise. I was due to start at La Boissiere in a matter of days.

"Only the best for my son," he said, rather too loudly, as we entered the large building that housed the academy in the centre of town. "They only teach the children of the crème de la crème, the very best of society!"

I wished the ground would swallow me up. Not that I didn't want the chance to learn swordsmanship and better horsemanship, but I wasn't so sure about the other classes. The only lessons I had ever had before were with my father; I was not looking forward to comparing what Latin and Greek he had taught me to the other boys. And we were also supposed to learn *dancing*!

Worst of all, I could not help noticing that apart from being at least a foot taller than most of the boys, and darker skinned to boot, I was a good couple of years older too. I could be sure of besting any of them in a fight, but I would stick out like a palm tree on a bare hill.

La Boissiere was an exceptional building of white plaster, gleaming and new. We walked through a pale painted hall, where boys looked at me sideways under their white-powdered wigs. I dearly hoped I would not have to wear one of those things. Father introduced me to the master of the academy – a round man with glasses balanced on his nose. His lip curled when he saw me, and I wondered if they wanted me here at all.

"You are Thomas-Alexandre?" the master said. I nodded, then Father left and I was hurried to the Salle d'Epée, which I gathered was the fencing class.

More sulky wealthy boys, dressed almost as flashily as myself, stood around the walls of the room and regarded me as if I were the dirt on their shoe. I tried to stand tall. The fencing teacher clapped his hands for attention and I have to admit I stared.

"Chevalier!" The master waved the fencing teacher over. My mouth had fallen open. Here was a man, not quite as dark skinned as I was, but who, from his features, must have shared the same parentage – black and white – as me. The first such man I had seen in this building, and he was not a servant but a teacher of these wealthy white boys.

"This," the master went on, "is the Chevalier St George. You may have heard of him, he is the foremost swordsman in all France."

The Chevalier nodded a bow. "In all Europe, sir, I think you'll find, and my title was a gift from our king..." He looked me up and down. "You are the new pupil? American, I think?"

"Saint-Domingue..."

"Well, well," the Chevalier said, and the master took his leave. "Take your place, young man, show me what you can do."

"Now?" I said, suddenly terrified. I realised all the boys in the room were watching.

The Chevalier took my hand and led me to the centre of the room and put up his sword.

"*En garde!*" He may have been a head shorter than me, and he may have had a face covered in powder and rouge, but he was fast – a blur of velvet and silver buckles. I parried, blocked – steel struck steel – and in seconds I was disarmed, my sword clattering to the ground. I hoped my face did not betray how surprised I felt – I had been told moments ago he was the finest swordsman in all Europe, and I felt ashamed to have underestimated him so badly on account of his appearance.

"Young sir," the fencing master said. "You are not as good as you think you are."

The other boys laughed.

The Chevalier waved them to be quiet and smiled, a kind smile. "You must be faster. Trust the blade."

I nodded, bent to pick up my weapon. "Again, sir," I told him. "Let me try again." I readied my blade, feeling the weight of it. It was not as heavy as Father's cavalry sabre, but thinner and lighter. I took up position. The fencing master looked hard at me, and then he turned to the class.

"You see this student?" He pointed towards me; I felt a flush of embarrassment. "He is tall and well built. There is some natural talent, but the épée?"

He signalled me to him and took my sword out of my hand. I wished the ground would swallow me up. "This is not his weapon." He made a face to the class, then looked hard at me. I was reminded of how Captain Langlois had looked me over and tried very hard not to think about it. The fencing master walked across the room and picked up a different weapon. It was larger, curved, a tassel of blue silk hung from the handle. "You might prefer a sabre I think?"

I blinked, nodded, and took the weapon. It was like Father's, only without the spots of rust. It felt familiar, comfortable. I turned it over in my hand and smiled. I would not make it easy for my teacher.

He bowed to me and I bowed back. I forgot about the other boys and tried to think only of the coming fight, that this sabre was somehow a part of my body.

"*En garde!*" he said again, putting up his blade, and came at me lightning-fast. Our blades clashed. He attacked. I blocked, and blocked again, and this time, when I felt the blade sing as I attacked, he stepped back. I had him. But then he was on me again, and even though I blocked and blocked, with a flick of his wrist he disarmed me again. My weapon crashed to the floor.

This time the boys watching did not laugh. But I felt just as stupid.

The Chevalier looked at me and his eyes bore into mine like needles. "You will see me after classes. No excuses. No lateness."

That afternoon when the other boys left for home or games by the river, I went to the gymnasium, where the Chevalier was waiting for me. How he managed to look down his nose at me when I towered over him I do not know. I expect it came from knowing his skill with a blade surpassed any other man in Europe. I took a deep breath and hoped he could not see I was a little afraid of him.

"Young *comte*," he said, and I could tell from his voice he was mocking me. He must have seen the frown on my face as he handed me the sabre. "Listen to me, young man. You have the capability and the promise to make a swordsman of the highest skill."

I did not know what to say. I was struck dumb. I had come ready for more humiliation.

"Like you, I came from the islands. Like you, I am a product of the new France. Like me, you have more skill with a sword than your entire class. But your life will be twice, maybe three times, as hard as any of theirs."

I went to speak but he put out his hand to stop me.

"For men like us, people of colour, it matters not whether we are counts or lords or knights. There will always be someone in our way, someone telling other people we are never good enough. They call us Americans, but they don't believe we should be free."

I nodded. I knew he was right. Even in my fine clothes, there were always a few who would mock me in the street, stare at me as I passed. I knew that none of my classmates, the elegant sons of dukes and earls and princes, had ever wanted for anything. None of them had ever spent any time as a slave.

The Chevalier went on. "So you will train three times as hard. With me, after class. Swords, épées, sabres, everything. You will be ten times as good as everyone else. And you will fight with grace and with honour at all times. In order to let that anger go, you will work and work and work until no one can best you. Are we clear?"

I could not conceal my enthusiasm. "Yes, sir!" I said, and saluted the Chevalier in the old style, sweeping off my hat and bowing like a musketeer from a storybook.

He smiled, then in one quick flowing movement threw me an épée so narrow and thin it might be a needle, and took the position, knees bent, his own sword in front of him.

"First of all, I teach you to disarm your opponent," he said. "Watch carefully. Believe me, young man, it could save your life one day."

His voice was fierce now, as he barked the order. "*En garde!*"

Chapter Six

1782, Paris

I loved La Boissiere. After three years I could gallop down enemies, riding without any hands on the reins if needs be, and shoot – and hit – a moving target. The other boys stopped challenging me to fights as they came to realise they would never win, and I sought out new opponents instead: adults, grown men. The Chevalier, delighted, often set me up with men he knew from the Royal Guard, and I hardly ever lost to them, either. I heard later that the boys made up stories about me, and some of them were so far-fetched I wondered how anyone would believe them.

Of course there were a few that concerned my skin – that I was the Chevalier's secret child, that I practised some kind of island magic. But the most ridiculous one, I quite enjoyed. It goes like this:

In the academy there was a covered riding arena, where we schooled the horses all year round, rain or snow or frost. The ground was sand, which we boys had to rake every day and the roof was held up with wooden crossbeams. More than once, I overheard the son of the Duc de St Gildas telling his friends that I was so strong that in a riding lesson he had seen me put up my hands to hold on to one of these beams, and lift up the horse I was on with my thighs!

I never corrected him.

My life at home was less exciting. My father never forbade me anything, but he could not look at me, and I thought – I hoped – that it was the weight of guilt at what he had done to his other children.

Sometimes I would think of them when I woke up in the night, and then I would lay there until morning, unable to close my eyes again. I would dream of Maman, and she would be weeping at what had happened to us. Then sometimes I would dream that I had my own money – piles of it – and I would send it back to my brothers and sister, only to find that they hated me as much as I hated our father.

And I did hate him. So much it burned, and so much that the words I needed to say to him would never come. He wished I would call him Papa again and laugh with him, but I couldn't. To me he was Alexandre Davy de la Pailleterie. The Marquis of Nothing. The Prince of Idiots. The man who sold his children for a title. And I wished more than anything that I wasn't his son.

I made up my mind to live my life as hard and as fast as I could. After all, I knew that one's circumstances could change in an instant; for all I knew I might go from young count to slave in the blink of an eye. So as soon as I finished at La Boissiere, I took the advice of the Chevalier St George and took rooms in Paris.

The relief at not having to see Father's face or be reminded where my wealth came from was pure joy. I am ashamed to say I bought the finest clothes and boots and blades money could buy; my father's money ran through my fingers like water, and I lived the life of a spoilt gentleman. I went to the theatre, I drank, I played cards. Some evenings I stayed up all night and talked politics with my friends in cafés – could there ever be freedom if some men were kings and others slaves? What made a Frenchman? How best to live a good life? Was being poor bad luck or one's own fault?

I was a count, my clothes were the best, the most expensive. I was exciting. I had many, many girlfriends.

Of course there were words thrown at me in the street occasionally; that was only to be expected. The Chevalier had been right, of course, but he had taught me well too. I won many duels, and I felt that in spite of how some men might look at me, the streets of the greatest city in the world were mine. But even so, things had begun to shift.

One evening I was sat at tables in the Palais with some friends I knew from the academy; Remy, whose father was a duke, and Fontaine, who had returned from travelling across Europe and thought he knew everything. We sat and debated freedom –

"How can France be proud of herself while her people languish in poverty!" I said. "In slavery!"

"Thomas, you are a dreamer." Fontaine waved me off. "The king is our king for a reason..."

"An accident of birth..." Remy chipped in.

"You agree with me!" I said and turned to Fontaine. "Remy agrees!"

Remy shrugged, though. "The English killed their king and then had to find another from Germany; perhaps someone has to do it."

"But do you believe in freedom?" I insisted.

"Freedom!" Fontaine laughed. "No man is free, any woman less so. Our situation is decided at birth, always has been."

"You believe a person born to slavery should remain so, then?" I said.

Fontaine shrugged. "If one is worthless enough to be enslaved, or born to a slave, what else is there?" He took a drink, he must not have seen my anger rising. "It is the same with poverty, my friend. Only a fool or a lazy man is poor."

"Did you learn nothing, man? On those travels of yours?" I was bristling. "You are the laziest man I know – if your logic follows, you would be the poorest too!"

Fontaine was scowling now. He leaned forward across the table, jabbing his finger at the tabletop. "I am an aristocrat. It is only what I deserve."

I should have shut up then. But I could not. "So a child born to a beggar, faultless, blameless, deserves nothing? In fact deserves to suffer?"

Fontaine shrugged. "It's natural law."

I took a drink. "That is not a world I want to live in."

"You cannot change it, my friend! Nobody can." Fontaine lifted his glass. "Freedom for some, perhaps. But I draw the line at freeing slaves or letting men vote; it is not natural and that's an end to it."

I shook my head. I suddenly felt tired and sad. I might have been a count, but what good was that, when there were so many titled men like Fontaine –

or like Remy, who agreed with me but would not stand firm and say so? I knew that Fontaine was wrong, that injustice could not simply be the natural order, but it would take so much more than one man if it were ever to be changed...

Suddenly there was the sound of breaking glass – I broke out of my thoughts to realise a man at a table across from ours was being set upon.

Before I could think, I was already striding across to stand between the man and his attackers, two small men with southern accents. And then, just as suddenly, the police had arrived.

One of the southern men pointed at me. "It was him, the big American!"

"I did nothing, sir! On my honour! I was only trying to help!"

But nothing I said changed their minds. It took Remy and Fontaine to protest my innocence before they agreed to let me go.

The young bloods were still arguing about politics and freedom as we left the café. I crossed the road in my finery and I thought that even though I had money and a title, they meant nothing. Why had I been so stupid as to believe a velvet jacket and fine manners might protect me from the poison within some men's minds? Wherever I went, whatever I did, my skin would always speak the loudest.

I was a fool to take my father's coins, to think wearing his name was anything other than a kind of disguise. What was the use of it? That title could no more persuade the police of my innocence than it could convince Fontaine and his ilk that other men my colour should be free.

I had told myself that I was spiting my father by spending his money, but really I knew all this time I had been pleasing him by eating from his hand. I had let myself grow comfortable on a lie.

No more, I decided. That night as I walked home, I resolved to change my path.

In June, I gave back the keys to my expensive apartment. I parcelled up my fine clothes and said goodbye to my horse, Gunsmoke, and I went to the army barracks to the north of Paris, where they were enrolling for the Queen's Dragoons. Even in my plainest clothes I looked richer than most, but I joined the queue of ordinary men waiting to join up. I had become twenty-four that year. Perhaps here at last I might be able to make some sort of a difference.

"American! Hoi! American!" A man pushed in ahead of me. "You won't last long in the Dragoons, the Spanish will see you coming a mile off!"

His fellows laughed, but I stayed put. "This is my country," I said. "And I will fight to prove it."

I felt in my pocket for the letter I had received from my father when I told him of my plans, and I took it out as I stood in line. I could almost feel his fury in the paper. He had summoned me home – he would cut me off! No son of his would join the rank and file as a private! A common soldier! I should be an officer! And the Dragoons? Cannon fodder! Food for sabres! Didn't my family tree go back five hundred years? Had he paid out all that money to the academy for nothing?

I hadn't replied.

At the head of the queue there was a table with a register, where we signed our names. The man who'd pushed in, took off his cap when he reached the front.

"Name?" The sergeant at the desk barked the question.

"The name's Jacques Piston," he said, "but I don't know my letters," and he signed an X instead.

"Next!" The sergeant looked up at me, pen poised. "Come on, man!"

"I can write," I said, and took the quill and dipped it in the inkwell. I took a breath, then wrote: *Alex Dumas*. The name my mother gave me. Now, even though her grave might be forgotten, she never would be. Every time they called my name – Private Dumas – I would think of her.

As I stepped away from the table I felt as if a weight had left my shoulders. My old name, my title – I had finally left them behind.

I took the letter out of my pocket and tore it up with a kind of giddy elation. The wind took the scraps of paper. I would never speak to him again, I decided then. I would be my own man now: plain Alex, son of Marie Cessette Dumas.

Thirteen days later, I heard news of my father's death. I did not attend his burial; I felt nothing at the news and wanted nothing he had left behind. I did not want to be a marquis. I was no longer a count. I was no longer a gentleman, and for the first time since Father sold me to Captain Langlois all those years ago on the island, I felt as if I was free.

Chapter Seven

1786, Laon, Northern France

Father had been right about one thing: the army thought we were disposable. The Queen's Dragoons were looked down upon, by the King's Own Dragoons especially, but by everyone else as well. We were a light cavalry unit, and in wartime we did the dirty jobs: taking out snipers, defusing traps, holding bridges until the regular troops could come through, and so on. In peacetime they used us against smugglers, against highwaymen.

But no amount of scorn from other regiments could make me regret my choice. At least they wore it on their sleeve! I felt alive for the first time in years and I made the best friends, not least Jacques Piston, the man who'd pushed ahead of me in the queue.

There was a camaraderie between us Dragoons that I had never felt with the other spoilt gentlemen's sons at the academy. We trained hard with our horses, and our guns. Louis Espagne called me "cowboy" after I galloped down after a band of smugglers, reins in my teeth, guns in both hands. I felt like that fourteen-year-old boy, galloping on the beach back home in Saint-Domingue, again.

Jacques had the measure of me. We were in an inn one evening, close to the barracks. I had rounded up a gang of salt smugglers and the wine was flowing.

"Our Dumas is a show-off!" he said, lifting his glass. "To Alex, the hero of the Dragoons!"

I did not argue. As I looked around at my new friends I thought they were more than simply mates or comrades. "To our new family!" I lifted my glass.

Louis cheered and filled the glasses again. "Another toast!" he said. "You think of one, Alex, you're better at this lark."

I stood up and thought a second, then raised my glass high. "All for one!" I said. "And one for all!" The inn resounded with all our cheers.

Suddenly the celebration stopped. A party of the King's Own regiment, our sworn enemies, had entered by another door. They looked at us as if we were no more than the turd on their boots. One swept off his hat and put it down on the bar, and he sneered at us as he ordered his drink.

"I see the queen doesn't care if Americans fight for her honour."

Jacques stood up. "He isn't American! He's as French as the rest of us!"

No lie, but I felt a prickle in my throat. I sat still for a moment. The king's men jeered.

"Can't the gorilla speak? Or is his head as empty as any one of your queen's men?"

I stood up, pushing the table away. "No one speaks to any one of us like that!"

The king's man at the bar sneered. "You talk like a posh boy but you look like a gorilla! Do they duel in the trees?"

I glared at my tormentor. He was almost as tall as me, and strong about the shoulders. He might have been a boxer for all I knew, but I reckoned my years with the Chevalier had done me good.

"You can talk to my blade!" I spat the words.

"You? A swordsman?" he said. He looked at me with disgust. I longed to wipe that sneer off his face.

"Right here," I said. "Now. Or are you afraid?" I took off my jacket. "If I am a gorilla, it will not take you long to dispatch me... *sir*." I said the word like a curse, and his face flushed.

The innkeeper hustled us out into the road, and we chose our seconds and lined up. I took my regimental sword and weighed it in my hand. It was nothing like the fine flashy blades I had learned with at La Boissiere, and I realised as I held it that it had been a long time since I had practised anything like a formal duel. Maybe I had made a mistake. My second, Jacques, whispered to me, "Are you sure? It's not too late to walk away..."

But I knew I couldn't. I handed Jacques my hat and smiled with a confidence I wasn't sure was mine, yet.

When I turned back, my enemy had his jacket off too. We faced each other, swords up. He was older than me, I reckoned, but not by much.

The shout came. "Fight!"

I let the sword guide me. He advanced and I parried, metal against metal. I looked into his hard grey eyes and thought of all the men who had ever wronged me, and I knew I could not let him win.

A crowd had gathered. I tried to shut out the sound. The king's man lunged towards me, his blade cutting the air next to my cheek. I only ducked out of the way at the last minute. I parried again, thinking of what the Chevalier had told me: I must work three times as hard. I attacked, he knocked my sword away and I felt a sharp sting on my forehead. Then the smell, a tang of metal that I knew was blood. He was smiling now. He had cut me. I had to wipe the blood from my face.

I saw Jacques' face, he looked afraid. I could not lose – not merely for myself, but for my comrades, my regiment. My brothers.

"We are not finished, sir!" I said, and put up my sword in readiness again.

The man sneered. "Do you want to die, American?"

I attacked, and he swatted me away. I gritted my teeth, tried to concentrate and remember my lessons. He came for me again, I parried – yes! Success – his blade turned away just in time. Then a twist of my wrist, a flick – my opponent's sword clattered to the floor. I stepped back. The crowd cheered.

I put out a hand. But his face was a picture of rage and indignation.

"Beaten by an American and a Queen's Dragoon," I said. The cheer that went up from my comrades sent the King's Own men scurrying back to their camp.

Or at least we thought it had.

We went back into the inn and called for more wine. But before we could open the bottle, there were two more challengers wanting to regain the honour of the King's Own Dragoons. They called me American – and worse, much worse.

"Alex, forget it, you have nothing to prove. We know who you are." Jacques poured me a drink and clasped my shoulder warmly. "One of us."

I took the measure of these challengers, one taller than me, one shorter. I was full of the confidence of victory. I looked round at my comrades at the bar. Jacques was not lying; they would not care if I didn't fight. But I did.

I stood up, and handed Jacques my hat and jacket. "Hold these. I bet you two sous I'll be back in a few minutes."

I slept sounder that night than I ever had in my life. I needed the regiment sawbones to put a couple of stitches in the cut on my cheek, which I received in the last bout, but I won every fight. Now the whole regiment knew me. I was a mascot; a lucky charm. And I was as French as the rest of them.

Chapter Eight
1789, Paris

In my time in the Dragoons I saw comrades die, not even in battle but in skirmishes, and what for? So our king and queen could sleep happy in their gilded castle? My comrades and I spent long evenings talking, about our betters, about the unfairness of the world. About why one man born in one place should have everything when others have nothing. There were no Fontaines here; we had all known hardship, and few of my brothers in arms had any illusions about suffering simply being anybody's deserved lot in life. Those who did think that way knew to keep it to themselves.

The wind was changing.

My regiment were in barracks to the far north of Paris, readying for a mission to catch a gang of smugglers on the border, when the shocking news reached us. After years of bad harvests and high bread prices, the French people – my people – had finally had enough of kings and princes and marquis and counts. The prisons had been opened, the newspaper said, and people were rioting in the streets. The king had been overthrown. A National Assembly had been formed to run the country.

It seemed as if those ideas of liberty, of freedom for all, which we had endlessly discussed, had at last begun to come true.

"Jacques, Louis!" I ran through the camp until I found my friends by the stables, seeing to our horses. "Listen to this –" I brandished the newspaper – "we are no longer subjects, we are citizens! We are free."

"Does that mean I can put my feet up?" Jacques said.

"Listen, this is important! 'All men are born free and remain equal in rights!'" I read aloud. I felt my heart growing full and perhaps, just perhaps, there was something in my eye. "All men! You and me, and every single one of us!"

I bought the wine that evening and we drank to liberty. I hoped that back on the islands, if they were still alive, my brothers and sister were free too.

We heard that the Palace Guard had decided to change their name: they were no longer protecting kings or queens, but their countrymen. They became the National Guard. We were still Dragoons, but now we fought for everyone, for all of France, and for liberty and equality.

Of course it was not an easy process. Upheaval and change brought with it a measure of chaos. Even posted as far from Paris as we were, we heard reports of looting and terror, of ordinary folk killed for no reason. But it was our duty as Dragoons to protect the citizens of France. In the summer of 1791, a nearby town called for help against looters, and twenty of us rode to their assistance.

The place was called Villers-Cotterêts, an old town on a hill. We rode in through the gates and were greeted in the square by the local mayor and a small crowd of townspeople. The mayor was also the local chief of the National Guard, he wore a tricolour cockade in his hat, the colours of the revolution – red white and blue.

He approached me first. "Citizen!" he said as he took off his hat.

Our captain sighed as he dismounted. "Just because he's taller than the rest of us doesn't mean he is in charge, sir," he said, a little annoyed.

"Ha! Forgive me." The mayor smiled. "I am Mayor Claude Labouret, innkeeper of the Hotel l'Ecu. But you may call me Citizen, we are all free men and women here."

Jacques looked at me, grinning. He took off his army hat and threw it up into the air. "*Vive la France!*" he shouted, and the all town – myself included – joined in. "*Vive la Republic!*"

I noticed a girl standing in the crowd throwing up her cap along with everyone else. She had brown hair and the kindest eyes I had ever seen. I soon found out her name: Marie-Louise Labouret, the mayor's daughter.

We were there for four months. It was a little like a holiday if I am honest. The town was on the main road, but Paris was a very long way away, and once word got out that twenty National Guardsmen were stationed here, the town's granaries and food supplies were safe from looters. We barely had to do any fighting. Over the summer we helped with the harvest, or with any chores, and on other days the townsfolk took us into the surrounding forest to hunt boar and stags.

I spent a lot of time with Marie-Louise and her family. I told her stories of Saint-Domingue, of the tiny hummingbirds that were so small and flew so fast their wings were a blur of jewel-bright colour, of the songs of the tree frogs, the warm sea full of flying fish, and of the sunsets. And during those summer months we fell in love. I knew more than anything that I wanted to marry her, but how could I? As a common soldier it would not be fair. I did not earn enough for two.

That winter, word came of war on the borders. Since France had given up her king, other countries were afraid the revolution might spread. The armies of the Austrian Netherlands were attacking on our northern borders. A messenger came – the soft life was over. We were to join the battle.

"Alex, I will wait for you." Marie-Louise walked with me into the entrance of the Hotel l'Ecu. She leaned close. "I promise," she whispered. My heart sang.

"We ought to speak with your father," I told her. "We must do this the right way."

Citizen Labouret was in his office. I knocked and we both went inside. He looked up from his desk and I must admit I was more afraid at that moment than I ever was before or after – whether faced down by a hail of gunfire or locked in a dungeon for year on year.

"Citizen Labouret." I coughed. I was almost strangled with nerves. "I have to ask a question, sir."

He put down his pen. "I am all ears."

"I..." Marie-Louise tugged at my arm. "I mean, we – we wish to marry. But I know... I know I am only a private, an ordinary soldier. Tomorrow I am off to the northern front. Marie-Louise has said she will wait for me. I ask – we ask – if you will allow us this marriage – if, and only if, I return at least a sergeant."

Citizen Labouret looked at me. The silence seemed to go on forever. I must be mad, I thought, to imagine he would want someone like me in his family! I held my breath.

But in an instant Citizen Labouret had stood up and embraced first me, then his daughter. "My boy!" He shook his handkerchief out of his pocket and mopped at a tear. "I cannot imagine a better son-in-law!"

We left for the border, I with a spring in my step, thinking of how best to impress my commanders and win promotion. It would be hard. I had to first become a corporal, then a sergeant...

As we approached the border we met carts carrying wounded men back southwards. I had never seen war first-hand, and I thought then that perhaps I would be lucky merely to return alive. I shook the thought away. What better fight could there possibly be? Freedom, my country, and now my heart's desire! I kicked my horse on towards the battle. However long it took, I would not let Marie-Louise down.

We were fighting for months. I became used to the smell of blood and the boom of cannon. Our unit was assigned to make raids on the enemy; I was put in charge of a group of four horsemen, Jacques and two others. We made camp in an old barn. Our maps said we were over the Belgian border and we felt twitchy, as if the enemy were all around.

"Build the fire smaller than usual, Jacques," I said as I unsaddled my horse. "We're too close for comfort."

We all spoke in whispers that night. I did not sleep. The ground was damp and hard, and every night-bird screech or fox rustling in the hedgerow kept my eyes open.

At last I gave up and woke the others. "Come on, if we start now, we might surprise the enemy."

We were all used to getting ready in the half-light, and soon we were riding out across the Belgian farmland.

We rode down a small track that ran along a ditch. On the far side of the ditch was a field planted with beans. The crop had grown tall; the war must have interrupted the harvest and the dry leaves rustled and crackled as we rode along the edge of it, a sea of stalks.

Suddenly my horse twitched his ears. I eased my weight down in my saddle to stop her, and put my hand up to signal my comrades behind me to stop. I listened. The world was still. A bird sung somewhere above. A wind rattled the dry leaves on the trees. And there was something moving in the bean field.

Suddenly there was a burst of sound as a Dutch raiding party galloped out of the crop and loaded up. Twelve men, mounted and armed. We started to turn our horses, but it would be no use.

"Too late!" I hissed. "Shall we die like cowards? Shot in the back?"

"There's too many of them!" Jacques called. "They will kill us all!"

I wheeled my horse around. They were out of range of my pistol, but if I could get near enough with my sword I could take a few with me.

"Escape with the others. I'll hold them off!" I kicked my horse into a canter. He was called Joseph, an army horse, solid and wide and yellow, hardly built for speed. But I knew I trusted him, and he trusted me. I had one chance to save my men.

"Alex! No!"

I sat deep and kicked on. "All for one!" I yelled. I did not stop to think if Joseph knew how to jump.

I leaned close to his neck and took my weight off his back, "Come on!" I whispered. Joseph sped up, my heart was in my mouth, but he cleared the ditch with metres to spare and landed squarely among the Dutch soldiers. I was so close I could see the worn gold braid on the nearest man's tunic, and see his calloused hand reach for his gun. I let out a yell. "For liberty! For France!"

I took my sword in one hand and lay about the beanstalks, cutting them down like a man on fire. A gunshot, a clear miss. I scythed through the beans with my sword. I couldn't stop now. Closer and closer – there was a man right in front of me, sunburnt, face worn from hard living. But I could see his eyes were tired. He was reloading, swearing. I had a chance. I spurred Joseph on, and when I was up against him, brought my elbow into his side – he crumpled sideways off his horse, gun and all. Behind me came another misfire and then the sound of a bullet hitting my sword, almost throwing it out of my grip.

Suddenly there was a yell. "Stop! *Arretez!*" Then the sound of rifles hitting the ground. I circled the men, counted twelve. They had their arms up. They were surrendering! It was over in seconds. The men dismounted.

I sat tall in my saddle and tried to hide the fact that I was shaking.

By the time Jacques came riding into the field I had twelve men sitting in line, their hands tied behind their backs.

We returned to camp heroes. Twelve prisoners, twelve horses, twelve Austrian-made carbine rifles, twelve army-issue sabres. Jacques stood me more wine than I could sink. Our captain wrote up a report – twelve prisoners, a record! – and I was promptly dispatched to Paris for a commendation. There would be, the captain promised, at least a medal.

I heard the news, as I rode to Paris, that the Republic was winning battles all along our frontier, freeing provinces of Belgium and Germany as we went. Our army was growing.

There was more than just a medal waiting for me in Paris. I was offered posts with two brand-new regiments, first as a sergeant with the Hussars of Liberty and Equality – and then I received a letter from my old friend and mentor, the Chevalier St George. I could not refuse. The Chevalier offered me the rank of lieutenant colonel, and the post of second-in-command of his new regiment, the Free Legion of Americans – the Black Legion. A band of men of all colours, fighting for equality. We took the name American and made it ours.

With the greatest swordsman as our commander, and with the hunger for equality that is known only too well to the oppressed, we would show France that our hearts beat for liberty too.

I met the Chevalier at the hôtel de ville in Paris. I bent down, and we embraced. "It is Colonel St Georges now, old friend."

"And I am proud to fight by your side," I told him. "But there is one thing I must do first, if you would give me leave?"

Of course he did. I returned to Marie-Louise in Villers-Cotterêts, and that November of 1792, we were married.

The Black Legion was like nothing I had ever experienced. It was almost like being at home. There were men from all over the islands, men from the United States, men who had been born free and men who had escaped the lash. We were like brothers. And as much as I missed Jacques and my other comrades in the Dragoons, it felt so easy being one of many instead of a rarity.

We were posted back to the Belgian border, doing the dirty jobs again – raiding and missions deep into enemy territory. My reputation grew, for while I was a commander, I always made sure I led my men to battle from the front.

Outside the world of war, France was changing faster than a spinning top. A school was set up in Paris where French children of colour and white children could have the very best education together. There would be liberty for all; the slaves on the islands would be free, in time. It truly felt like anything was possible.

There were even new names for the months, the days of the week. I was happy to be a citizen, to be a part of something new, something fair. But France's enemies had grown in number; not only the Austrians, but Spain, Portugal, Naples and Great Britain stood against us.

Colonel St Georges became less involved with the regiment as the war wore on, and the day-to-day running of it became my affair alone. And an American legion was sadly treated less than fairly by the Ministry of War. We suffered with supplies not being sent and wages not being paid. Some of our best fighters left for the islands. More than once I imagined joining them, returning to the warm sand where I had grown up.

But I stood fast in my duty to defend our newfound liberty. And in the summer of 1793 I received a letter signed by the Minister of War. I had been promoted, Brigadier General of the Army of the North, and then by the end of September to Commander-in-Chief of the Army of the Alps. I was no longer at the head of ten, or even a hundred men, but tens of thousands. I was responsible for them, and most importantly I felt personally responsible for the fight for freedom and liberty for France. Our country.

I had a few days at home with Marie-Louise and our baby daughter before I had to leave again. She helped me on with my uniform, the blue jacket of the National Guard, the discreet gold braid that denoted my rank on my shoulder, and the tricolour of the revolution on my hat, a cockade of red, white and blue.

Marie-Louise kissed me. "You look..."

"Ah, this is nothing, you never saw me in my finery," I laughed. I adjusted the jacket. "Although I think I would rather wear this than any of the finest silks or velvets in all the world." I had gained this rank on my own, without the advantage of name or title. I couldn't help feel my heart swell.

"Your father... What would he think of you now, do you think?" she said to me, picking up little

Marie-Alexandrine, named for both of us. I had told her about my father; she knew how furious he had been when I had first enlisted with the Queen's Dragoons.

"I don't know, Marie," I said, and bent to kiss the baby. I thought, not for the first time, that it was my duty to be a hundred times the father than mine had been. "But my mother – *she* would be proud. From slave to general? Who ever would have thought it?"

"And now all Europe stands against our country. You will stay safe, won't you Alex?"

"I promise."

"I am so scared, the stories from Paris... So many are dying. And it seems as if every country in Europe is out to fight us."

"We will win, Marie, we have to win, we have to stay free."

She nodded and I gave her a hug. Whatever happened in Paris, I told myself, I could not fail.

Chapter Nine
Winter 1794, The French Alps

I had never seen snow until that first winter in France when I was fifteen. Back home on the islands the sun was always hot, the sea always warm, and even the highest mountains were free of frost and ice.

But now I had been ordered to defend my country against Austria and her royalist Italian allies, the kingdom of Piedmont-Sardinia. Their king was intent on crushing our revolution and restoring the monarchy. We had to win.

My mission was to take the two well-guarded alpine mountain passes, Mont Cenis and Petit St Bernard, either side of a glacier – a massive river of ice – and so let our French armies cross the mountains into northern Italy.

This was a landscape I had never even dreamed of as a child, and now I was to lead thousands of men across miles of mountains to fight for our lives in winter.

I recruited Jacques Piston and Louis Espagne, from the Dragoons to fight alongside me. My second-in-command was General Sarret. We had an operations room, with a large map table in the centre, where we met to discuss our plans. Louis unrolled a map of the mountains and I traced the outlines of the passes, tiny dashes that showed the way from France into Italy. General Sarret was frowning.

"It looks impossible," I said.

Jacques clapped me on the back. "Come on, Alex! If anyone can do it..."

"The enemy will see us coming from miles away," Sarret said.

"My friends," I said. "I have an idea. Remember last week I went up with some local mountain guides? They wear white smocks so they are unseen in the snow."

Louis smiled.

I nodded. "I have already ordered enough for our fighting divisions to wear over our uniforms."

"How many forts?" Sarret asked.

"Here, and here." I pointed them out. "I have been up there to look. They have cannon and guns all ready and waiting."

Jacques Piston whistled. "We will need a miracle."

"And thousands of snowshoes," I said. "The snow is so soft, men and horses will fall through. We have to wait until the weather turns."

Sarret looked at me. "Is there no other way?"

I shook my head. "This is it." I said.

"The Ministry of War will not be pleased," said Sarret. "We need to march on Italy as soon as possible."

"I will not risk my people's lives." I stood up. "We wait."

And so our army waited for the spring. January passed, and February, and a letter came from the Ministry of War – I had been reported as a traitor to the revolution. I complained, and luckily the mayor of Grenoble stood up for me; he told them I was still a patriot and loyal to France.

I wrote back to the Ministry of War and told them in a letter that my soldiers were my brothers. I would fight for freedom but I would not throw lives away.

In April, when the worst of the snowfall was over, I took a division to take the Petit St Bernard pass, and General Sarret went to Mont Cenis.

It was still bitterly cold up in the mountains. Our uniforms were not made for such ice and snow.

The frost bit hard, some men lost fingers and toes. The climb was treacherous, and our horses' hooves slipped on icy mountain paths. I was almost at Petit St Bernard, where we had captured a fort on the road, when Jacques Piston rode one-handed into camp, his horse exhausted, his shoulder bandaged up.

"Sarret is dead. Him and three quarters of the men." He shook his head, his beard was still full of snow. "It was a massacre. The Italians had reinforcements. They simply cut us down."

I poured my old friend a drink. It felt as if my heart was breaking.

"I have never seen anything like it, Alex." Jacques looked at me. "The blood on the snow, I thought they were red flowers at first. Like poppies." He laughed bitterly. "Until I got closer." He took a drink. "They had spies. They knew we were coming. We walked right into a trap," he said. "They cut us all down..."

I shook my head.

"We have to take the St Bernard Pass, for all those men." I said. "For France and for a future free of kings. We owe them that."

"The men are tired, Alex," Jacques said. "You need to find a way to remind them what this is all for."

The climb up to the St Bernard Pass was long and hard and very cold. The path for the horses was narrow, and many times we had to dismount and inch along narrow ledges with ice cliffs on one side and sheer drops on the other.

I could not fault my men. In the face of hard cannon fire we reached the top of the pass with no losses and barely thirty men injured. In fact the enemy seemed struck down with surprise that we were there at all. The Sardinian soldiers melted away into the spring snow and we took their positions easily, raising our flag for liberty on the roof of the world.

Once we had secured the pass I set off with my men for Mont Cenis. We would not let them win. This time we kept our plans top secret. I knew the Sardinians would not expect another attack, and this time we would make some key diversions along the mountain ridge close by. I would take the fight to our enemy as if I was in a duel; make them look the other way while I disarmed them.

I made sure we had every bit of weaponry, grenades, even clubs and pikes. Every man had a bayonet – a sword blade fixed to the end of his army musket. In early May we began another climb.

The pass was defended on three sides, the enemy had – we knew – doubled their forces and had set up fortified redoubts that would cut down anyone approaching across the glacier. They had set up cannon and guns all waiting for us.

If you have never seen an Italian cannonball you might not understand the damage they can do, so let me explain. After they career headlong across the battlefield obliterating any soldier they contact, they can also bounce, indeed the gunners are trained to set them to bounce; and a ton of iron bouncing at one's head or chest means instant death. This is what we were to face, not simply the cold and the thin air of the mountaintops, but the chance to be mown down.

I would not let it happen again.

I had planned several small diversions and false attacks to distract the enemy and draw their fire – one to the left of the pass, the other along a ridge to the right. I sent Jacques Piston with a small force of men to set off explosions all along the ridge. For a moment, as I lay in hiding with the main attack force on the glacier, I worried nothing would happen. We waited. All was still and quiet; nothing moved, no wind, no birds.

Then the afternoon exploded again and again as the bombs went off. I waited until the Sardinians began to fire their cannon in the wrong direction. Then I stood up and led the charge across the sea of ice.

My men did not let me down. We ran, we slipped, we snowshoed across the glacier, climbing ridges and stumbling through the snow. We had a good ten minutes before their guns rained down straight at us to get to the smaller fortress.

I saw one of my men brush off a broken leg. "It's nothing!" he said as he hauled himself up into a captured fort. Another, whose hand had been blown off, kept going, firing with his good hand. Every single one of us fought like furies.

We scaled the walls, set grenades against the walls and stormed inside. The Sardinians, surprised by our speed, surrendered. Then we turned their guns on the bigger fortress and fired their own cannon across the glacier at the enemy.

I knew my men would not give up. We were fighting for Sarret and our fallen brothers, for liberty and for equality. We would not stop until victory was ours.

The Sardinians retreated away down the mountainside and back to their king. We would have chased them all the way to Turin.

We took nine hundred prisoners that day and captured forty cannon, and by a miracle we suffered only seven dead and thirty injured. Every man was a hero.

Jacques Piston found me later that evening in the fort at Mont Cenis. I was looking west across the mountains. The sun was setting, and the snow was the same colour as the inside of the shells I used to find on the beach in Jeremie long ago.

"We did it, Alex. Nine hundred prisoners, and the rest running back to their king in the south." He took two metal cups and set them out on the table, filled them with the local brandy we'd found in the fort's cellar.

"Seven of our brothers dead," I said and wished we had not lost any. I looked out across the mountains again. Breathed in the sharp clear air that tasted of freedom.

I thought of my brothers and sister. Of my young family, of the new France. I was fighting for all of them, for the moment when there would be no slaves and when all men and women could stand equal. I felt a prickle in my chest. Jacques clapped me on the back. He raised his cup.

"To the seven," he said. "And to liberty!"

"To liberty!" I said and gulped the brandy down. "To all of us across the earth."

Afterword

This was not the end of Alex Dumas's incredible life, but it was the beginning of the end. There was a young Corsican officer, who took the opportunities the revolution gave him and rose up through the ranks almost as quickly as Dumas. His name was Napoleon Bonaparte. Napoleon was jealous of Dumas's success, and as he rose he looked for ways to have Dumas demoted.

Dumas became a military governor in northern Italy, where he is remembered for his sense of fairness and honour. He was recalled to the army when Napoleon staged an ill-judged invasion of Egypt, to free the Egyptians from their Mamluk rulers. The Egyptians assumed Dumas, as commander-in-chief of the cavalry, was the French leader, which annoyed Napoleon even more.

The invasion ended in disaster for France – but not before Dumas, in yet another feat of bravery, saved local Egyptians from a coup. Napoleon had a painting of the glorious victory commissioned, but he made sure that the saviour galloping to the rescue was not Dumas.

As Dumas returned to France, the ship he was on put into Sicily, where he was captured by the king and detained in a dungeon, without any charges or chance of freedom. Dumas's incarceration lasted nearly four years. He was poisoned and his health suffered in the damp stone castle. He was able to write home, though, and his wife and supporters petitioned the king and the French government to release him.

Eventually, in 1801, Dumas made it back to his wife and daughters in Villers-Cotterêts. He wrote continually to Napoleon to be paid for the time he spent in prison, and looking for a new commission. But Napoleon ignored his letters.

Dumas had one last child, a son, in 1802, but died in 1806 when his son was only four. This son, also named Alexandre, grew up to be one of the most famous and popular French writers in history. He wrote thrilling adventure stories, inspired by tales he had heard about his father – a man who could fight three duels in a day, who believed in honour and equality, and who was imprisoned for no reason.

His books are still in print today. You might not have read them, but you'll have heard of them: *The Three Musketeers* and *The Count of Monte Cristo*, among others.

One of the few letters that remains from Alex Dumas, is this one, to his men before the battle for Mont Cernis. It gives a measure of the remarkable man who led a life so incredible it formed the basis for some of the most well-loved stories ever written:

"Your comrade, a soldier and general-in-chief ... was born in a climate and among men for whom liberty also had charms, and who fought for it first. Sincere lover of liberty and equality, convinced that all free men are equals, he will be proud to march out before you, to aid you in your efforts, and the coalition of tyrants will learn that they are loathed equally by men of all colours."

READING ZONE!

TOP READING TIP

When reading an historical novel
it is often a good idea to make
yourself a timeline to work out
when it is set and how the events
fit in to history.

The events in this book take place
in Saint-Domingue (now Haiti)
and France but you could find
out what was happening in
other countries too.

READING ZONE!

WHAT DO YOU THINK?

If you had to describe him
Alex to someone what words
would you use?

Do you think giving up his
money and position and working
up through the ranks was the
right thing to do?

What do you think his father
would really have thought of
him by the end of his career?

What about his mother?

READING ZONE!

QUIZ TIME

Can you remember the answers
to these questions?

• What were the names of Alex's
younger brothers and sister?

• How much money did Alex's father make
by selling his son to Captain Langlois?

• What were the colours of the revolution?

• What job did the Chevalier St George
offer Alex in his new regiment?

• Who was Alex's second-in-command
in the French Alps?

• What was the name of the
woman who married Alex?